Bear Dreams

Elisha Cooper

📖 **Greenwillow Books**
An Imprint of HarperCollinsPublishers

Bear can't sleep.

Why do the other animals get to play outside

while he has to stay in a cold cave, sleeping?

It's not fair.

Bear has an idea.

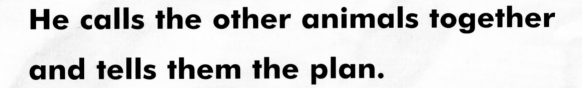

He calls the other animals together
and tells them the plan.

"I want to race," he says.

"I want   to

climb

trees."

"I want to fly across the lake

and then fly back."

"What if we get tired," the animals say,
"and want to rest?"
But Bear says, "No!"

Shhh . . .

Bear sleeps.

His mother and father carry him

back to the warm cave,

where he will sleep until spring.

For Mia

Bear Dreams Copyright © 2006 by Elisha Cooper. All rights reserved. Manufactured in China. www.harperchildrens.com Watercolors and pencil were used to prepare the full-color art. The text type is Futura Bold. Library of Congress Cataloging-in-Publication Data • Cooper, Elisha. Bear dreams / by Elisha Cooper p. cm. "Greenwillow Books." Summary: After a bear cub persuades his friends to play with him instead of hibernating, he gets very tired and falls asleep. ISBN-10: 0-06-087428-7 (trade bdg.) ISBN-13: 978-0-06-087428-5 (trade bdg.) ISBN-10: 0-06-087429-5 (lib. bdg.) ISBN-13: 978-0-06-087429-2 (lib. bdg.) [1. Bears—Fiction. 2. Hibernation—Fiction. I. Title. PZ7.C784737 2006 [E]—dc22 2005034349 First Edition 10 9 8 7 6 5 4 3 2 1 Greenwillow Books

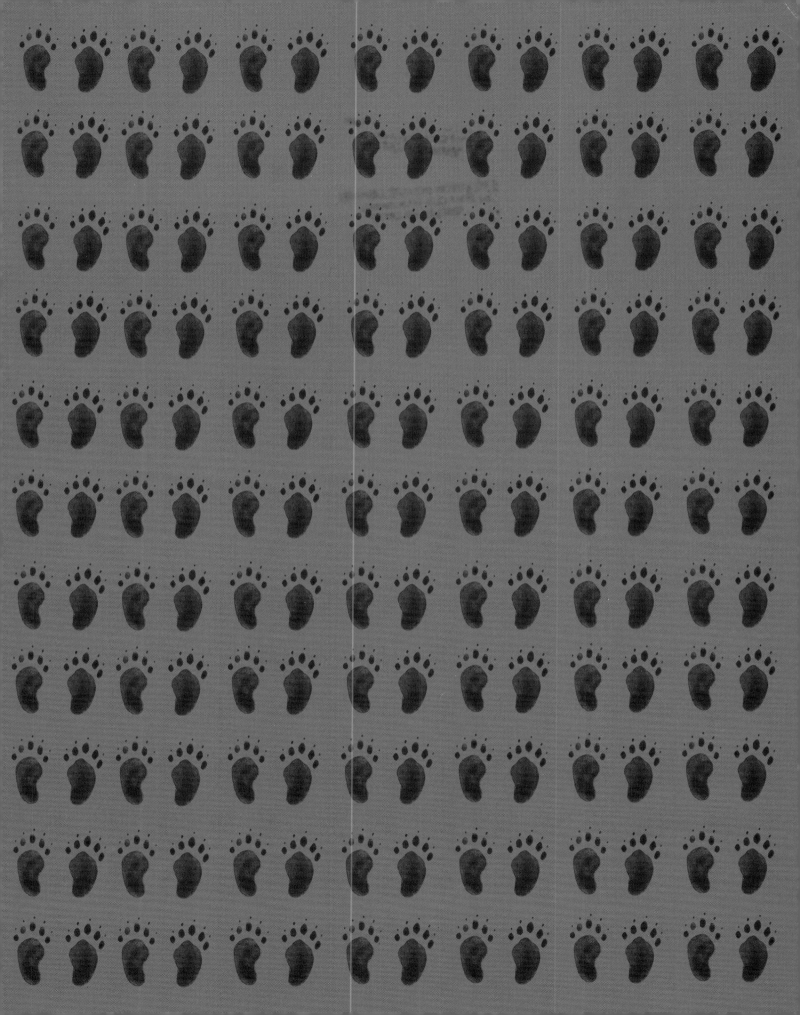

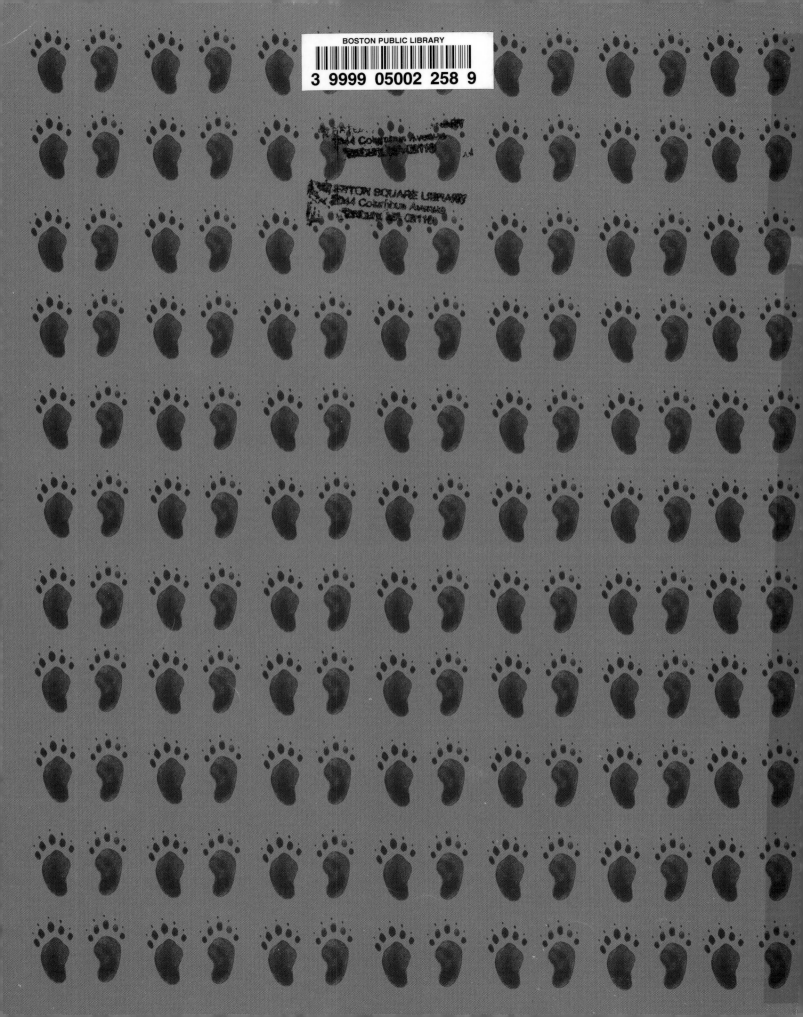